To Josephine   L.G.

Text copyright © 1991 by Libby Gleeson

Illustrations copyright © 1991 by Armin Greder

First published in Australia in 1991 by Ashton Scholastic Pty Limited as *Big Dog*

The illustrations were drawn with pen and ink and colored with liquid acrylics.

The text type is Berkeley Old Style. Printed in the United States of America.

Library of Congress Cataloging in Publication Data

Gleeson, Libby. [Big dog] The great big scary dog/by Libby Gleeson; illustrated by Armin Greder.

1st U.S. ed. p. cm.Originally published: Big dog. Sydney: Ashton Scholastic, 1991.

Summary: Jen decides to deal with her fear of a big dog by scaring him back, but
her attempt has an unexpected result.[1. Dogs—Fiction. 2. Fear—Fiction.]

I. Greder, Armin, ill. II. Title. PZ7.G48148Gr 1994 [E]—dc20 93-13398 CIP AC

ISBN 0-688-11293-5 (trade). ISBN 0-688-11294-3 (lib.)

First U.S. edition, 1994

10 9 8 7 6 5 4 3 2 1

The GREAT BIG SCARY DOG

Libby Gleeson

illustrated by

Armin Greder

TAMBOURINE BOOKS • NEW YORK

There's a big dog on our street. My sister Jen is scared of it.
She hides behind me when we walk past on tiptoe. She's even
scared when we walk past with Mom. When the dog barks at
Jen, she cries and runs away.

Mom says it can't jump the fence but Jen is still scared. I tell
her it can't crawl under the gate, but she's *still* scared.
"I hate that old dog," she says.
It's very embarrassing.

Dad says to ignore it. Mom says to look the dog in the eye and keep on walking. Cindy, who lives with us, says to walk

on the other side of the road, but we aren't allowed to cross the street by ourselves.

"What can we do?" I said to my friend Diep.
We were painting a dragon for our New Year's dance.

She put the dragon's head on and roared.
"We could scare the dog," she said.

We practiced at our house.

ROAR!

Dad was so scared that he stepped back onto a roller skate
and nearly fell on top of the baby. Mom jumped up in the air
and banged her head on the cabinet.

Cindy nearly fell off her ladder.
She gave us red and gold streamers to hang from the dragon's head.

We practiced on the front steps.

ROAR!

Diep's mother got such a shock that she turned the hose on
the man next door.

He got such a fright that he dropped his groceries and was crawling in the gutter to pick them up.

We went out the gate, Diep in front, then Jen, and then me.

We planned to go to the dog's house, stand on our side of the fence, and roar so loudly that the dog would be scared right out of its wits.

Diep stopped. I couldn't see what the problem was.

"What's going on?" I said.

"The dog," said Diep. "It's out of the yard. It's on the path."

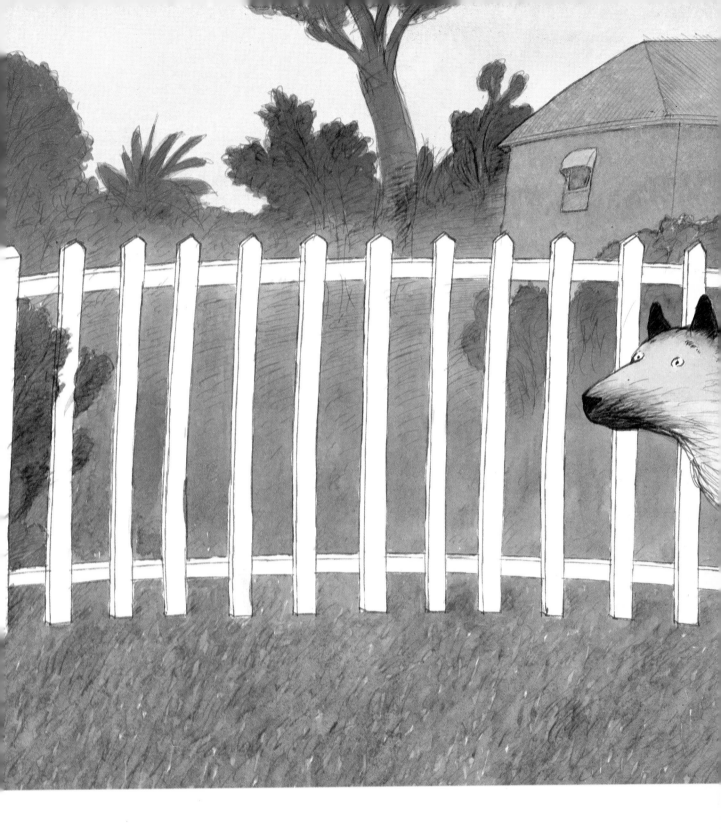

Jen started to cry. She tried to turn around but she was stuck under the huge sheet.

"It's coming toward us," said Diep.

I felt a bit nervous myself.

"Keep still," said Diep. "It's almost here."

The dog sniffed her feet.
Then sniffed Jen's, then mine.

"Pet it," said Diep. She knelt on the grass and put her hand out to the dog. I peeped through a hole in the sheet. The dog lay on the grass and let her stroke its forehead. I touched its back.

It put out its wet, pink tongue and licked the dragon's face and made a happy, gurgly sound. After a minute, Jen stretched out her hand and gently touched the top of its head. The dog rolled over and rubbed its back against the grass. We tickled its tummy.

When we got home, Mom said,
"Well, did you scare that old dog?"

Jen nodded,
"We sure did," she said.

Now, when we walk past the house down the street, the dog opens one eye and looks at us in a lazy way.

Sometimes it runs to the fence and, just for a minute, Jen holds my hand. Then she calls out in a loud voice, "Roar," and that old dog just wags its tail till it looks like it might fall off.